My Sister Is Sleeping

Devora Busheri

Illustrated by Michel Kichka

KAR-BEN
PUBLISHING

My little sister, achoti, is sleeping.
Her eyelashes look like tiny
feathers lined up in a row.

She is little.
She is sleeping.

Soon she will wake up.

Mommy, Ima, will put her in my lap
and I will giggle with delight.
When I offer her my finger,
she will grab on tight.

Her hands, *yadayim*, open like paper fans.
She is sweet.
Sweet and sleepy.

Soon she will wake up.

Mommy will give me a bowl and a spoon, k'arah v'kapit, and I will feed her oatmeal. Yum!

Her lips are like two little strawberries, tootim.

She smells clean like milk, *halav*.

Now she is sleeping
but soon she will wake up and open her eyes, einayim.

Mommy will put her in the stroller, agala, and I will take her out for a walk.

I am already a big girl.

Posing for the camera

The sand is hot!

First driver's licens

Eating ice-cream
in Tel Aviv

I lost my first tooth!

Congratulations!

19

My little sister is sleeping.
Soon she will wake up.

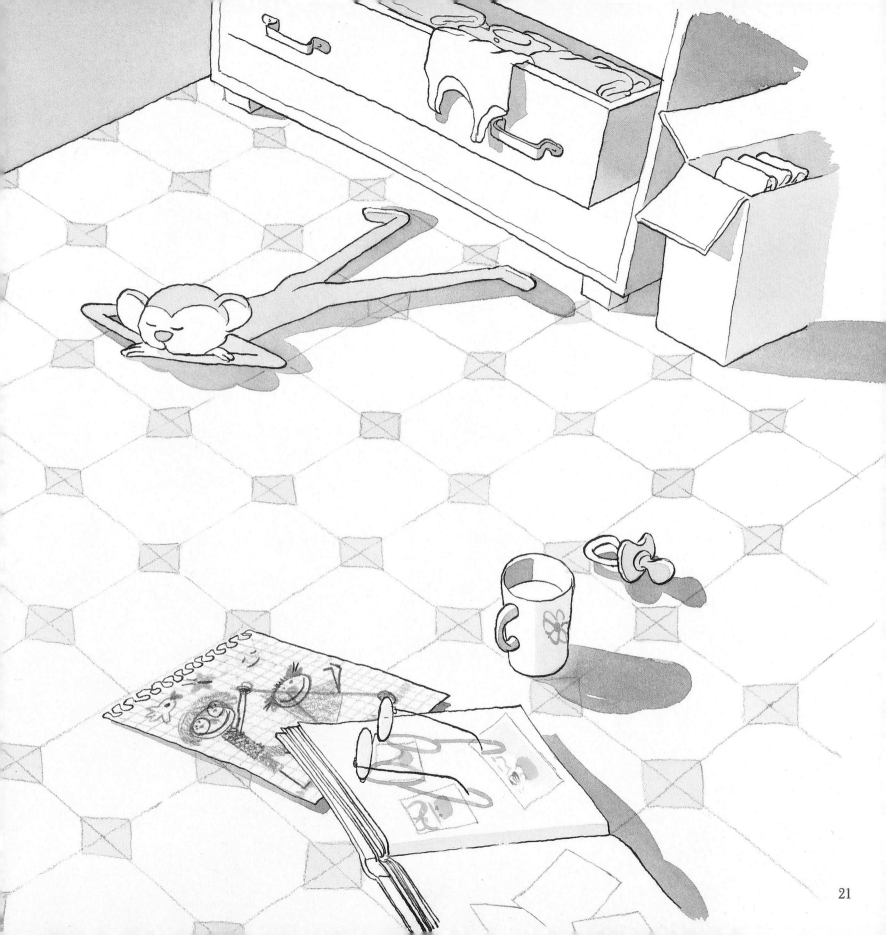

KAR-BEN PUBLISHING, INC.
An imprint of Lerner Publishing Group, Inc.
241 First Avenue North
Minneapolis, MN 55401 USA
1-800-4-KARBEN

Website address: www.karben.com

Main body text set in Varius 2 LT Std.
Typeface provided by Linotype AG.

Library of Congress Cataloging-in-Publication Data

Names: Busheri, Devora, 1967– author. | Kishkah, Mishel, illustrator.
Title: My sister is sleeping / Devora Busheri ; illustrated by Michel Kichka.
Description: Minneapolis : Kar-Ben Publishing, [2020] | Series: Israel | Summary:
    "An older sister dotes on and admires her precious baby sister, weaving in sweet
    details in English and in Hebrew"— Provided by publisher.
Identifiers: LCCN 2019007486| ISBN 9781541542440 (lb : alk. paper) |
    ISBN 9781541542457 (pb : alk. paper)
Subjects: | CYAC: Sisters—Fiction. | Babies—Fiction. | Family life—Fiction. |
    Jews—Fiction.
Classification: LCC PZ7.1.B8877 My 2020 | DDC [E]—dc23

LC record available at https://lccn.loc.gov/2019007486

Manufactured in the United States of America

1-45410-39523-6/4/2019